Hi, My Name is
Frankie

WRITTEN BY
Lyn Fontinell

ILLUSTRATIONS BY
Jade Pinto

ISBN: 1451544340
ISBN 13: 9781451544343
Library of Congress Control Number: 2010903651
CreateSpace, North Charleston, South Carolina

For my son
and all the children like him.

Hi, My name is Frankie.

What
is your
name?

I am in the second grade.

What grade
are you in?

I do ok in math and writing,
but my favorite subjects are
reading, gym, music and art.

What are your favorite
subjects at school?

Sometimes I don't want
to go to school.
I just want to hang out
and watch TV.

Do you ever feel like that?

I have a lot of video games!
I love to play them when
I am at home.
I am pretty good.
Mom thinks I play too much,
but I don't think so.

What do you like to do
when you are at home?

I really love to eat
cheese burgers!
Once in a while
Dad brings home
a kids' meal for me.
It makes me upset
when the toy in the box
was not the one I saw on TV.

Has anything like that
ever happened to you?

The park is fun!
I like the swings.
When other kids are there
I have to wait my turn.
I don't really like to wait.
My Dad says, "Be patient,
you will get a chance."

Have you ever had to wait
for something fun?

I am afraid of
really dark rooms.
Mom put a night light
in the hall so I
can see a little.
It makes me feel better.

Are you afraid of anything?

When someone
asks me a question, I can
have a hard time getting
the right words out.
That really makes me
feel embarrassed.

Have you ever felt embarrassed?

When I am very excited
about something,
once in a while
a funny noise comes
out of my mouth.
I can't help it,
it just pops out.

Have you ever made
a funny noise?

Hey, you know
we have a lot
in common.
We all have things
we like and don't like.

That's cool!

We may have one
difference though.
I have autism.
It's not contagious.
That means you
can't catch it from me.
I have had it since I was very little.

Having autism may make
me think a little differently
than other kids sometimes.
But that's ok;
I still love video games
and cheeseburgers.

Hey,
I bet you probably know
some kids like me
in your school or
in your neighborhood.
They may not talk like you
or do all the same things
you do, but I bet you
have lots of things in
common with them too.
They may surprise you!

Next time you see
someone like me
why not go up and say;

"Hi! My name is ...."

And they might say,

"Hi! My name is Frankie."

Wouldn't that be...

A NOTE FROM THE AUTHOR;

Thank you for sharing this book with your children.
Statistics show that 1 in every 88 children are diagnosed with autism (according to data collected by the CDC). Chances are that your children will come across someone with this disorder in his or her lifetime. He or she may see a child whose behavior is difficult to understand. This child might make funny noises or have repetitive movements, may not utilize age-appropriate speech (if any speech at all) and may not make eye contact. Your child may be afraid to approach these children because what they see is different; and different can be scary. Let's open a dialogue and let all children know that someone with autism is not flapping their hands or making noises because they want to, but because their brain or body tells them it is a necessity. Underneath what is seemingly different is a child with the same feelings as any other. They have likes and dislikes; they can feel sad or happy, disappointed or embarrassed. We need to take away the fear of autism and replace it with knowledge. If given a chance, there could be friendships formed that will enhance the lives of not only the children with autism, but the lives of all children. Celebrate the differences, stress the similarities and take away the fear. Thank you again for taking a step and sharing this book with your children. Together we can make a difference.

Lyn Fontinell

Made in the USA
Charleston, SC
20 December 2012